I Like to Read® books, created by award-winning picture book artists as well as talented newcomers, instill confidence and the joy of reading in new readers.

We want to hear every new reader say, "I like to read!"

Visit our website for flash cards, activities, and more about the series:
www.holidayhouse.com/ILiketoRead
#ILTR

Phonics features of this book—**cvc:** big, new, has; **cvce:** home, makes; **long vowels:** beach, needs, snail, trail; **digraphs:** fish, beach, shrimp; **variant vowels:** all, more, move, moves, new, too; **blends:** wants, help, helps, friends, snail, crab; **sight words:** a, and, are, go, here, is, the, too, we; **story words:** jammed, octopus, seahorse, friends.

Guided reading level: D

OCTOPUS MOVES

Bob Barner

HOLIDAY HOUSE • NEW YORK

Octopus wants to move.

The beach is jammed.

The fish are too big.

Here we go.

Snail makes a trail.

Shrimp helps.

Crab helps.

Seahorse helps.

Octopus needs more help.

More help is here.

All the friends help.

Octopus has a new home.

And a new friend.

I LIKE TO READ is a registered trademark of Holiday House Publishing, Inc.

Text and illustrations copyright © 2025 by Bob Barner
All Rights Reserved.
HOLIDAY HOUSE is registered in the U.S. Patent and Trademark Office.
Printed and bound in December 2024 at C&C Offset, Shenzhen, China.
The artwork was created with paper collage, gouache pastel, and pencil.
www.holidayhouse.com
First Edition
1 3 5 7 9 10 8 6 4 2

This book has been officially leveled by using the F&P Text Level Gradient™ Leveling System.

Library of Congress Cataloging-in-Publication Data

Names: Barner, Bob, author, illustrator.
Title: Octopus moves / Bob Barner.
Other titles: I like to read (New York, N.Y.)
Description: First edition. | New York : Holiday House, 2025. | Series: Like to Read | Audience: Ages 4–8. | Audience: Grades K–1. | Summary: "When Octopus needs a new home, this community of sea creatures is on the move and ready to help out"— Provided by publisher.
Identifiers: LCCN 2024005016 | ISBN 9780823458158 (hardcover)
Subjects: LCSH: Octopuses—Juvenile fiction. | Helping behavior—Juvenile fiction. | Readers (Elementary)—Juvenile fiction. | CYAC: Octopuses—Fiction. | Helpfulness—Fiction | Reading (Elementary).
LCGFT: Readers (Publications) | Picture books.
Classification: LCC PZ7.B2597 Oc 2025 | DDC [E]—dc23
LC record available at https://lccn.loc.gov/2024005016

ISBN: 978-0-8234-5815-8 (hardcover)

EU Authorized Representative:
HackettFlynn Ltd,
36 Cloch Choirneal, Balrothery,
Co. Dublin, K32 C942, Ireland.
EU@walkerpublishinggroup.com